# & the Dragon

*written and illustrated by*

TONY DiTERLIZZI

SIMON AND SCHUSTER

## *Acknowledgments*

Tony would like to thank

ANGELA, KEVIN, ELLEN, ARI, SCOTT,

STEVE, JOHN, JENNI, HOLLY, and WILL.

In memory of

GOBLIN DITERLIZZI

(1994–2006).

Your love and inspiration will

always live in our hearts.

**SIMON AND SCHUSTER**
First published in Great Britain by Simon & Schuster UK Ltd, 2008
A CBS COMPANY

This paperback edition published in 2009
Originally published in the USA in 2008 by Simon & Schuster Books
for Young Readers, an imprint of Simon & Schuster
Children's Division, New York.


Book design by Tony DiTerlizzi and Lizzy Bromley.



1 3 5 7 9 10 8 6 4 2

Simon & Schuster UK Ltd, 1st Floor,
222 Gray's Inn Road, London WC1X 8HB

A CIP catalogue record for this book is available
from the British Library

ISBN 978-1-84738-502-4

Printed by CPI Cox & Wyman, Reading, Berkshire RG1 8EX

*For my little girl,*

SOPHIA.

*It's what's on the inside*

*that counts.*

# *Before I Forget . . .*

*Many years ago . . . Hold on, I know what you are thinking. You're thinking a book about a dragon should start with "Once upon a time." But this one doesn't, because frankly, I don't really know what "Once upon a time" means. Now, I was* once upon *a horse, and that was fun. Also, I was* once upon *a knight galloping on his horse, but that's another story altogether.*

*So instead, let me start our tale with this:*

*Once upon a farm, in a town just west from yours, and on a Wednesday many years ago, a rabbit farmer, his wife, and their son, Kenneth, were preparing to sit down to supper.*

*Now, Kenneth seems a little formal for a boy's name, doesn't it? No kid would say "Kenneth, can I borrow a pencil?" No, they'd say "Ken" or "Kenny, can I borrow a pencil?" And no doubt our Kenny would not even notice when they swiped it from his school desk, for you see, Kenny always had his head buried in a book.*

*And he loved to read all sorts of subjects: science, mysteries, histories, and even fairy tales. In fact, fairy tales and natural history were his two favorite topics, and as far as Kenny was concerned, both held the same merit in the real world.*

*So it is not surprising that he enjoyed going to school. He always asked compelling questions, always did his homework (complete with footnotes and a bibliography), and always had fantastic notions about what he wanted to do when he grew up.*

*One day he'd want to be an astronaut and meet extraterrestrials from a distant planet. The next he'd decide on a jungle explorer looking for living dinosaurs, or he'd build a submersible that could go deep in the ocean to find lost underwater cities. Each day it was something new.*

*"That kid has such an imagination," his English teacher would say.*

*"His identification of local flora and fauna is quite impressive," his science teacher would say.*

*"Kenny Rabbit? He's kinda out there," his classmates would say.*

*And to a certain degree, they were right. You see, like them, Kenny grew up on a farm, and both his mother and father were farmers. They came from generations of farmers who grew vegetables and raised livestock. So his parents, like most of his neighbors, really didn't have time to read books—they were just too busy tending the farm.*

*"You can't harvest corn with a book," his mom would say.*

*"No booky book's gonna bring the sheep in at sundown," his dad would say.*

*Regardless of what they thought, though, his parents did their very best to support Kenny in all that he did, right down to listening to his lengthy theories on this and that over dinner.*

*"You see," Kenny would tell them, "it's going to rain because cold air and warm air collide in the upper atmosphere. This creates thunder, and it causes the moisture within the cumulus clouds to fall."*

*"I thought it was going to rain because the cows are layin' down," his dad would reply.*

*And most folks in town would have agreed with Kenny's dad.*

*Hold on a second . . . what was the name of that town? I can't believe I've forgotten. It was near water, if I recall correctly.*

*Dunhill? No, that's in the northern province. . . .*

*Meadow Falls? That's not it either; but it was a stream or a river. . . .*

*Roundbrook? Yes, that's it! The town was sort of roundish in layout, with a brook running through the middle of it. (Goodness, I can't believe I'd almost forgotten—not something a fellow in my position should allow.)*

*All right, then, so in the little farming town of* Roundbrook, *Kenny lived with his parents, went to school, did his chores on the farm, and filled the rest of his time reading, which is precisely where we find him at the beginning of our tale.*

# I. That Devil Scourge

KENNY'S FATHER BURST INTO THE kitchen, panting heavily. His ears twitched. It was suppertime, and Kenny's mom was making her family's favorite, corn chowder. The soup's heavy aroma swirled about as the farmer moved through the room.

"Pack all yer things! We're outta here! We're moving!" Kenny's dad hollered. He was a scraggly, hairy fellow wearing a wide-brimmed hat, and he was trying to catch his breath, as if he'd been running.

"Moving? Not now, mister," Kenny's mom

replied. "The corn's not boiling yet, the broth isn't quite right, and I still have to sew the patches on Kenneth's trousers for school tomorrow."

Kenny's dad paused, walked to the stove, dipped a finger in the pot, and agreed it still wasn't quite right.

"Get your dirty paws out of my chowder! Wash your hands, have some milk, and tell me what's got you so riled up." She ground a little pepper into her broth. Unlike Kenny's father, she was soft, round, huggable, and seemed to always be adorned in an apron with a spoon in hand.

Kenny's dad did as he was told. Then he stroked his ears and started:

"This afternoon my eyes saw something I wish they'd never seen. I went to shepherd home the flock up on top of Shepard's Hill, where they had been a-grazin' all day. As soon as I get up there, I sees the sheep all huddled and quiet on the far side of the hilltop, and I think to meself, what in the world has got 'em so spooked? So I wander over to the other side of the hill, you know where them rocks and boulders are?"

"Mm-hmm. Here, taste this. Better?"

"Yes, much better. So I—"

"Hold on, dear. Kenneth! Get out here and set the table."

The wooden floorboards creaked as Kenny shuffled into the kitchen, his head buried in his book. He was reading a story about a giant, written by a man named Oscar. Without looking up, the small, skinny lad opened the cupboard and grabbed plates to place on the table.

"Not plates—bowls, Kenneth. I told you earlier we're having corn chowder tonight. Get your head out of the clouds, put the book down for a minute, and set the table properly." His mom snatched the book out of his paws and set it on the counter.

The wooden counter was dinged, scratched, and stained from years of use. Pots and pans hung from the ceiling, right above where Kenny's mom was cooking. She reached over and opened one of the numerous round windows to allow the cool country air into the kitchen.

"Don't you want to hear the rest of my story?" Kenny's dad whimpered through his milk mustache.

"Of course, dear. Of course. What did you find in the rocks?" his mom said as she tasted the soup.

"So there I am, climbin' up on them big rocks and boulders. All the while I'm thinkin' there must be a wolf, a lion, or a bear hiding in there. Remember I said I heard those weird whooshin' sounds coming from the hill last week?"

Kenny folded the napkins and placed them around the banged-up wooden table. "I remember that," he said. "I thought—"

"Hold on, son, hold on," his dad interrupted, waving his hands about. "So I make some noises of my own to see if I can spook it off. And that's when I saw it."

Kenny stopped setting the table and looked up. "Saw what?" The gears in the lad's brain began to turn. He realized his father's tale involved some sort of encounter with a carnivorous animal. Kenny figured he could determine just what his dad had seen based on the description. A lion was out of the question—they were too far east for lions. Wolves usually traveled in packs and were rarely seen in these parts, but bears did prefer rocky outcroppings and caves. . . .

"Well, first I smell something burning. Not wood, but something smokylike. Then I see a pair of glowing eyes, and then a head, as big as this here table, peers out from an opening in the side of the hill, and it's covered in horns and scales and fur like a crocagator."

"You mean *alligator*," Kenny corrected him, though he wondered what sort of alligator had horns and fur.

"Exactly, but have you ever seen a *blue* alligator? With a neck like a turkey, and a body like one of them giant lizardy things in your books?"

"You mean dinosaurs, Dad? Those really did exist, you know. Scientists have even found their bones in old—"

"No, son. This wasn't one of them *Brontosaurus rex*es." His father looked him in the eyes. "It was like one of them flying things that eats pretty maidens and burns castles to the ground."

Kenny paused for a moment. *It can't be*, he said to himself. *It couldn't be*. He put the last of the silverware in its place on the table.

His father just sat there staring at him with his big eyes. Glancing over at his mother, Kenny noticed she had stopped cooking and was looking at them quietly while holding the ladle. He turned back to his father. "Dad, are you talking about a dragon?"

"Yes, son. I am talking about one of them dragons." He started pacing around the kitchen, waving his arms wildly. "It's taken up residence on the side of Shepard's Hill, and we gotta sell the farm and move before that devil, that scourge, comes down and burns everything right to the ground."

## *II. Dishes and Homework*

"NOT IN A MILLION YEARS," KENNY'S mom said. She then blew on her spoonful of soup and sipped it up.

"But *Mom*! It's a dragon! I wanna go see it before anybody else does!"

"Who knows what that thing could do to you? You could get bit, or scratched up, and it's probably carrying all kinds of diseases. Right, Pa?"

As usual, Kenny's father was much calmer now that he had eaten, and Kenny studied him as he started on his third bowl of chowder. The dainty wooden soup spoon looked odd held in his rugged, worn paws.

In fact, the lad half waited for his father to lift the bowl up and slurp the remainder of the chowder. Instead he calmly said, "If Kit thinks he can handle the likes of a dragon, then I think we should let him. After all," he continued, winking at his son, "he ain't no little bunny anymore."

His mom folded her napkin and set it on the table. She sighed. "All right, but not until you finish the dishes and your homework."

"Awww! I can do those later. Lemme go now, pleeeease!"

"Dishes and homework first," she repeated as she pointed at him with her spoon.

Kenny cleared the table and cleaned the dishes in record time. As he finished drying the last of the soup bowls, he watched the sun sink lower and lower in the darkening sky.

When he was finished, he ran into his room and dumped his book bag upside down onto his bed. Textbooks spilled out, pencils rolled off onto the floor, and loose papers scattered like white leaves. Kenny shuffled through it all and picked up *Stars and Their Constellations*, the book he was supposed to do a book report on. It was his last assignment for the school year, and it would be an easy one for him, as he'd read the astronomy text front to back several times already—now he simply needed to write the report.

*Or*, he thought, *with a little persuasion on my teacher, Mrs. Skunkmeyer, I could do an oral report instead, and I won't have to write anything . . . so technically, I'd be finished with my homework.*

However, an oral book report meant going in front of the class and talking. The last time Kenny had done that, it was on the topic of "The Migration of the Ruby-Throated Hummingbird" for his science class, and it hadn't gone so well. One of his classmates had started snoring loudly, and another hooted, "Snoring! Boring!" bringing snickers to the entire room as Kenny tried to give his presentation. The other kids just didn't get excited about the stuff that he did. But honestly, who wouldn't be fascinated by the idea of a tiny bird flying all over the world by itself? If a little hummingbird could do that, well then . . . He paused in his thoughts, for there on the bookshelf, next to his copy of *Amazing Hummingbird Stories* was an old bestiary he had borrowed from his friend George.

He grabbed the leather-bound tome and

opened it up. It smelled musty and old, and in one whiff, Kenny was back in George's dim bookshop in a beat-up armchair, surrounded by stacks of books. Even though the shop appeared messy, it was quite organized. Yet only George knew where everything was, as he hardly ever left his little literary sanctuary.

When Kenny would visit, the retiree would always recount a story about his past adventures, usually over a game of chess, and he had plenty of new and interesting books to show. Many times he would let Kenny borrow books from the store as long as he took good care of them and returned them in their brand-new condition once he was finished. Sometimes he'd just let Kenny keep them as a gift.

Kenny flipped through the yellowed pages of the bestiary. Albatross . . . bear . . . chimera . . . "Dragon!" he said aloud. Kenny hadn't finished this book yet and had read only some of the entries. The illustration for the dragon showed a vicious, sinewy, coiled monster belching white-hot flames.

*An actual dragon*, the young rabbit said to himself. *It's like seeing a living dinosaur. Imagine bringing him to class for the science fair.*

He turned the page, and there were more pictures. One was of an armored knight fighting a dragon. In one hand the knight held a shield, in the other a long lance, with which he was pinning the reptilian beast down to the blackened, scorched earth. Fallen knights littered the background. A little gear in Kenny's mind clicked into place. "Maybe I can do my report on this bestiary instead—and add my own field observations," he said, slamming the book shut and shoving it into his worn leather book bag. "I better get prepared."

Dashing through the house, Kenny grabbed a pot, a pan, some rope, an old broom, and a garbage can lid. He strapped the blackened frying pan to his chest using the rope and his belt. Placing the pot on his head, he rolled up the sleeves to his flannel shirt and grabbed the broom, the lid, and his book bag as he headed for the door.

His mother and father were sitting in their rockers on the front porch. His dad was smoking his after-dinner pipe, while his mom was stitching a patch onto the knee of Kenny's trousers. Without looking up, she said, "I'm glad those are play clothes you're in. Homework finished?"

"Yes, Mom," Kenny replied, taking a lantern and hooking it to the handlebar on this bike.

"Be careful, Kenneth. I hope you know what yer doin'," his father said. He sucked on his pipe and rocked slowly in his chair, watching the sun set. "And tell that varmint not to eat any of my sheep."

Kenny turned to his dad as he climbed onto his bicycle. "I'll be fine, Pop. This is most likely an Olde-World wyrm. They're cold-blooded, so they are very slow once the sun goes down. I can outrun him any old day, should it come to that. Either way, I aim to find out just who he is, where he came from, and what his intentions are."

"Don't be out too late," his dad replied, but Kenny had already sped out of sight.

# III. *Grahame Like the Cracker*

KENNY LEFT HIS BICYCLE AT THE foot of Shepard's Hill, near Parrish Creek, where he waved to "Old Pops" Possum, who was at his usual fishing spot. From there he began hiking to the summit on foot. The weight of his makeshift armor made progress difficult as he worked his way past the oak and maple trees scattered about on the grass-covered

hillside. This hill, the largest in the area, had been on his family's property for as long as he could remember. He'd collected butterflies and wildflowers here last summer, read *The Wind in the Willows* under the large willow tree at the top last fall, and had sled races down the side on the garbage can lid he now held as a shield. It was his prized "snow saucer," and it had the scrapes and dents to prove it. Perhaps the dragon would take these marks, along with the blackened pots and pans, to be victorious badges of previously slain drakes—and would be respectful of the little buck. Perhaps the beast would even be a little scared.

Kenny made it to the grassy top by sunset. From here he could see the little lamplights of Roundbrook flickering along the horizon. To the west, billowy clouds changed in hue from gold to a fiery orange, then turned red before cooling off into a lovely shade of lavender. As Kenny looked east, he could see the North Star, Polaris, twinkling low in the sky. Directly below, curled up and sleeping on the far side of the hill, was the dragon.

He gulped. This animal was bigger than the illustrations in his book.

Much bigger.

Mesmerized, Kenny slowly approached the monster, happy to be downwind of it on the off chance that it could smell him and attack. He was halfway across the hilltop, when he thought the creature had sensed him because it was growling in a long, low tone—just like a lion. A giant, reptilian, bloodthirsty lion. Kenny froze, hoping it would stop and go back to sleep. But the beast never moved, and he soon realized it wasn't growling at all. *It was purring.*

"The book didn't mention anything about purring," he whispered to himself.

He pulled the bestiary out of his book bag and studied the picture once again. The image depicted a dragon that was slithery, scaly, and very fierce-looking. Kenny then looked up at the specimen in front of him. It was a bit rounder, and hairier, and scruffier, than what was drawn in the bestiary.

Kenny held his breath and strained against the gathering dark to see every little detail of the magnificent monster dozing in the twilight. He didn't dare make any noise, even though he was dying to light his lantern for a better view. After a while, the rhythmic purring started to make him feel relaxed. He listened while its large ribs expanded and contracted with each breath. He closed the book and put it into his satchel.

At this movement, the great beast cracked opened one large, lemon-yellow eye.

Kenny froze, mouth agape.

The creature's head rose up from the ground and focused on the small rabbit studying him. Then the dragon did a sort of a fake stretch and a pretend yawn and settled back down. (Of course, you know this move very well. It's the "I-am-pretending-to-fall-asleep-but-I-am-really-wide-awake" move, and is best used on parents when they check on you in your bed at night.)

The dragon closed his eye, gave out a sigh, then said in a low gravelly voice, "No throwing rocks at me, or poking me with a stick, or yelling at me, 'cause I won't tolerate it. And don't waste your time pouring water on me to douse my fire, 'cause that doesn't work at all. I just got comfy on a nice cool spot of grass here, and I'm trying to sleep, so leave your food and off you go. . . ."

The dragon's words trailed off and he began

fake-sleeping again, making a purring-sort-of-snoring sound.

Kenny cleared his throat. "Ahem."

Nothing.

"Erm. A-hem!"

Still nothing.

He had to try another tactic. Were all dragons this unresponsive? No wonder they were practically extinct.

"Cough-cough."

"Bantling, aren't you here with an offering? A meal and libation, perhaps? Leave it by my entryway, and then you'd best scurry home. It's getting late."

"I—I—I didn't bring you anything," Kenny stammered.

"No food?" the dragon said, not moving a single scale. "Then why on earth have you brought those pots and pans? Surely you were planning on cooking me a delicious dinner"—he eyed the garbage-can-lid shield—"and serving it on that large metal platter."

Not only had his book not mentioned dragons purring, it hadn't mentioned bringing gifts, either.

Clearly the author did not take his subject seriously, or else he hadn't done his research thoroughly. Kenny set his broom-lance on the ground. "Well, I do have a bestiary that I've been reading . . . but now I'm not so sure of its accuracy."

"A bestiary? Really?" The dragon's eyes opened wide and he quickly sat up. He rubbed his scaly paws together. "Come on, then, let's have a look." He extended his hand. It was nearly as big as Kenny was, and ended in long, sickle-shaped claws.

The young rabbit pulled the old book out of his satchel. He grabbed the ribbon bookmark and opened the book to the page titled "Dragons." "Please don't burn it. I'm borrowing it from a friend of mine."

"Burn it? What sort of unchancy firedrake do you take me for? Why, I'd just as soon burn my own tail as burn a book." He looked at the title on the cover, *The King's Royal Bestiary*. "Hmmm. Let's see here what it says."

The dragon stretched out his long, curly tail and reached it into an opening hidden in the shadows of the rocks and boulders on the hillside. From there, he pulled out a pair of metal-framed spectacles and set them on the furry bridge of his nose. To the lad, they were the size of dinner plates. Kenny removed the pot from his head and slowly sat down on it. He didn't want to make any quick movements, but he was ready to bolt in case the beast showed any signs of aggression.

"Wouldn't you just know it, a book arrives and there's nary the light to read it in. Do you mind lighting your lantern?"

"Uh, okay," Kenny said. "Sure." As he lit the lantern, fireflies began flitting about the top of the hill. They quietly blinked around the monster's giant head, revealing a jagged, toothy grin as he studied the pages.

Giving his best performance as a relaxed visitor, Kenny sat back down on his pot and plucked a stalk of grass. Casually chewing it, he asked, "How long are you here for?"

"Hard to say . . . ," the dragon muttered, flipping through the pages. "Hmpf!" he then snorted. "Rubbish! Well written, but the facts are not at all right."

"How do you mean?" Kenny asked.

"Look here. It says, 'A dragon's strength is found within its long and dangerous tail. Tying the

tail in a knot will render the foul beast harmless. But be warned, all drakes kill anything they catch with their vicious coils.' Not true. Do you, little bantling, kill everything you encounter?"

"Why, no," Kenny replied. He was wishing that the pot was on his head after all, and he gripped his garbage-can-lid shield tightly.

"Exactly," said the dragon. "But I could easily say that the general populace pretty much destroys everything they come in contact with—they certainly do when encountering a fellow like me. And *I* am not killing *you* at this moment, am I?"

Kenny thought about this for a bit. Was it some sort of trick? His heart was beating fast, and he was ready to take off, leaving everything behind. His parents, of course, would be quite upset at him for abandoning the cooking pot and lantern up on the hill. Certainly George would be cross as well, and Kenny didn't have the allowance to replace the bestiary he was borrowing. He looked up at the dragon, "You're not killing me at this moment. No."

"Nor do I intend to. The truth of the matter is, I've never killed a thing in my life," the dragon said as he closed the book and eyed Kenny.

"That was the fashion many years ago with the other dragons. They were so *earnest*, you know, burning down castles, fighting knights, and eating bedizened princesses. That was never my cup of tea. I am more what you'd call a 'Renaissance fellow.' I like to see the world and savor it, not destroy it. So, instead of burning down a castle, I would admire its architecture. Instead of fighting a knight, I'd challenge him to a good game of chess. And I'd never eat a princess. Instead I'd create a wonderful flower arrangement for her—to match the silk drapes in her palace, of course."

"Really?" Kenny said. This dragon was certainly not at all what he'd expected. Not a scourge, a devil, or even a nuisance.

"Well," said the dragon with a sigh, "that was how I got by: Live and let live. Which was all fine and dandy until I got trapped."

Kenny set down his garbage-can-lid shield and loosened the frying pan tied to his chest. "Go on."

"It took me completely by surprise. You see, I was snoozing under a tree, very much like this willow right here, when the ground literally opened up and swallowed me."

"A fissure," Kenny said. "You must have been in an earthquake! Whoa!" He stood up on top of his pot. "How did you survive?"

"I drank lava and ate firestones—which allowed me to breathe fire for the first time ever. Of course, they also gave me horrendous heartburn, which I still have to this day, but that doesn't matter, because the lava and firestones saved my life."

"They did?"

"Sure. I sat there under the earth and . . . well actually, I caught up on my beauty sleep first. So I *slept* there under the earth for years and years, but I kept dreaming of life up here—the glorious sunsets, the whispering trees, the birds singing gaily, daffodils . . . oh, and crème brûlée." As he said this, the dragon rose to his full height, causing the swarm of fireflies to swirl and dance around him. As the drake looked up, Kenny followed his gaze to the sky, which was so bright from the Milky Way that he could not tell where the fireflies ended and the stars began. The dragon took in a deep breath, then looked back down at Kenny. "And so I finally awoke. With my fiery breath, I blasted and burned a tunnel back up to the surface to see it all again. I mean, how could I miss all of this? That's when I arrived here."

"What a tale," Kenny said. "What do you plan on doing now that you're here?"

"Not much. Enjoy some fresh country air, eat a good meal, catch up on my reading, and write some poetry. Actually, I consider myself quite a poet. Would you like to hear some poems? I tried to recite a bit to an older chap who was up here earlier today, but he scurried off. Even after all these years, I suppose I can still have that effect on someone."

"That was my dad," Kenny said. "You scared him good."

"Scared him? Goodness! Was my rhyme that bad?" the dragon asked.

"I don't think you understand your situation." Kenny sighed. "You're considered a 'devil' and a 'scourge' to society. Just like it said in that book. Folks usually want to hunt you down."

The dragon put a claw over his mouth and let out a smoky snicker. "Hunt me? For what? Improper etiquette? They are the ones writing horribly inaccurate dragon facts in their books. It should be *me* who is hunting *them* down."

"But you don't—"

"Ken-NETH!"

The call rang out across the pasture from the direction of the farm.

"That's my mom. I gotta go or they'll be worried. Besides, I gotta get ready for bed," Kenny said as he grabbed his lantern. "Can I get my book back, dragon?"

"Grahame," the dragon replied. "My name is Grahame—just like the cracker, except with an 'e' at the end. And it was great chatting with you, um . . ."

"Kenny. Well, Kenneth. But everybody calls me Kenny."

"Well, Kenny," the dragon said as he handed over the makeshift lance and shield, "do come up again and bring your folks. In fact, let's do dinner tomorrow night. You bring the food, and I'll supply the entertainment. Is your mom a good cook? Tell her I have a ravenous appetite for soufflé, glazed carrots, mashed potatoes, and of course, crème brûlée."

"Oh, okay, I'll ask," Kenny said. "And the book?"

"Oh, please let me give it a read tonight. How I *love* good fiction."

With that, Kenny dashed back down the hill and hopped onto his bike. Excited, he pedaled toward his house. He couldn't wait to tell his parents how curious, how interesting the dragon whose name happened to be Grahame truly was.

## *IV. You're All Right in My Book*

IT WAS GETTING LATE NOW, AND Kenny's mom was pacing on the front porch, awaiting her son's return. Kenny's father was untroubled by the lateness and reminded her that they should trust their son's judgment on matters concerning nature and fairy tales.

And, as Kenny coasted in out of the darkness and into the yellowy porch light, he knew it was going to take some work to convince his folks to go up and meet Grahame. So he got to it immediately upon his return. He recounted, in great detail, his conversation with the dragon.

During his bath, he told his mom, "He was swallowed up in an earthquake centuries ago, where he survived by drinking lava and eating fire rocks. But it's okay, he won't burn me."

As he climbed into bed, he told his father, "Grahame says there used to be dragons everywhere, eating people and burning castles, but don't worry, Dad, he won't eat me."

And, at breakfast the next morning, he told both his parents, "He likes to read, and recite poetry, and eat crème brûlée. I can't wait to see him again!"

"I am thrilled to hear you've met someone you get along with so well, Kenneth," his mother said as she flipped a fourth helping of pancakes onto his father's plate, "but if you're planning on spending more time with that dragon, then I think it best that your father and I go up and meet him too. Don't you think so, Pa?"

"I do indeedy," his father replied as he sipped his coffee. "As long as this isn't some plan to eat my sheep, my son, or us, we are all on the same page."

So after school, and after his father brought the flock in for the day, the family trotted up to the top of the hill with picnic baskets in hand to meet Kenny's new acquaintance.

As they neared the grassy summit, Kenny's father stopped them all just short of the hilltop. He leaned on his walking stick and sized Grahame up while slowly chewing on a stalk of grass.

The large, blue-scaled creature was arranging the boulders at his cave entrance. He'd step back and study them, then adjust one here, and another there, then step back and look at them again. Finally he noticed Kenny and his family watching him.

"Arrah! Ho there!" Grahame said with a toothy grin. "I was tidying the place up for your visit."

Kenny's father put his paw on his son's shoulder and spoke first. "So yer not the type of fella to be deceitful to my li'l boy and trick us all into yer belly?"

The drake's eyes went wide, and he let out the slightest gasp. "Goodness gracious, no," he replied, "but I may trick you into reciting a favorite poem. If your son's a chip off the old block, I would imagine you are a fellow connoisseur of the spoken word. Yes?"

Kenny's dad just stood there chewing on his stalk of grass. The dragon looked at Kenny for a sign, but the boy just shrugged. At last, his mom grabbed his father by the arm and smiled at Grahame.

"We are very delighted to meet you, Mr. Dragon. Thank you for not eating us. I think you'll enjoy my cooking much better, anyway." She turned to Kenny. "Kenneth, dear, help me set up the picnic blanket."

"Please allow me," Grahame said, and walked

up to offer assistance. In doing so, he inadvertently stepped right on Kenny's father's foot. His father didn't utter a word—his large eyes said it all.

"I am terribly sorry, sir," Grahame said, then hiccuped. A small fireball puffed out of his mouth, engulfing the farmer. Kenny's father looked down at his son as the last of his singed eyebrows fell to the ground. The boy kept his mouth shut tight, barely suppressing his giggle.

"Oh goodness!" the dragon said, covering his mouth. "I—hic!—am a bit skimble-skamble today. And when I get nervous, I—hic!"

Kenny's mom took her apron off and wiped the ash from her husband's face. "Kenneth," she said, "get some cool water for your father's foot. It should keep the swelling down."

"There's that creek—hic!—at the foot of the hill," Grahame said as he took the bucket that they'd used to carry refreshments. In the dragon's scaly hand it looked like a little drinking cup. "Let me go—hic!—get it." With that, he bounded off.

"I don't want any whining, Pa," Kenny's mom said, putting his hat back on over his singed hair. "You'll be fine. Besides, you're making him as nervous as all get-out."

With Kenny's dad comfortably soaking his foot, dinner was served. Spread out on the gingham picnic blanket was a delicious meal of radish soufflé, sweet glazed carrots, and parsleyed potatoes.

The dragon squealed. "Oh, I haven't had sweet morsels like this in a long, long time!" Then he grabbed the entire bowl of carrots and tipped them over his open maw.

"Hey, mister!" Kenny's mom thumped Grahame with her wooden ladle. "Mind your manners."

"My apologies," he replied, gently placing the bowl back down on the blanket. "It's just that this spread is spectacular, and the mouthwatering aroma took complete control of me." The dragon winced with embarrassment. Kenny chortled.

As they enjoyed their supper, Grahame told Kenny's mom the stories he'd heard of the grand meals that royal chefs cooked each day for the king. He even gave her a few recipes.

The crème brûlée, torched expertly by Grahame using his left nostril, was delicious. Kenny's dad smoked his after-dinner pipe, while Grahame recited several of his favorite poems above the twitter of chirruping crickets. As Kenny watched the lights flicker on in the town below, he thought it was one of the best dinners ever.

"Well, Mr. Grahame," Kenny's mom said, "we

must be getting back. I've a kitchen to clean and a boy to get to bed. After all, this is a school night."

"Understandable, milady. Thank you all so much for coming up and visiting," said Grahame. "It was a magnificent meal." He turned to Kenny's dad. "I apologize for the foot. I trust it will be okay?"

"I'll be just dandy, dragon." He paused for a moment, stroking his whiskers. "You know, being that this here hill is on our property, you can stay up here as long as you'd like." He knelt down and gathered their dinnerware. "Jus' watch yourself. Folks may not take a likin' to a dragon livin' in these parts."

"Mum's the word."

"So long, Grahame," Kenny said as he shook hands (well, claw) with him. "See ya tomorrow?"

Both the dragon and the young rabbit looked over at Kenny's parents.

"Oh, of course," his mom said, "but Pa is right—be careful."

School the following week was not as exciting to Kenny as it had been before he'd met the dragon.

Summer break was fast approaching, and every class was packed with end-of-year merriment. Even so, Kenny couldn't wait to get home so he could spend the remainder of the day with his newfound friend.

Every afternoon Kenny went up to visit the dragon on the hill. On the weekend, Kenny's mom invited Grahame to have dinner at their house. But since he was far too large to come inside, they decided it was best that he simply put his massive head through their kitchen window, where a place was set for him at their table.

The following Tuesday was the last day of school, and the students were let out early. Kenny rode his bike as fast as he could to the top of Shepard's Hill so that he could tell Grahame about his day. He found him sitting in front of an old upright piano, wires jutting out from the top like dead stems in a flower vase.

"Ho, bantling! Look what your mom found in the barn. I think I can get it working again too," Grahame said as he pulled on a string and gently tapped a key.

"Neat," Kenny replied. "Hey, I received my grade for my book report today."

"And?"

"Well, my teacher was fine with me switching books. She knew I'd read *Stars and Their Constellations* before, anyways. But I'm not sure what she thought of me debunking the facts in *The King's Royal Bestiary*. She felt that those scholars must be the best in the land—after all, they were hired by the king."

"King, schming. What does he know?" Grahame replied, tapping another key.

"Exactly. I told her that unlike the author of the book, I had a firsthand account of what a *real* dragon was like."

Grahame stopped hitting the piano keys and looked at Kenny. "What did she say?"

"She said I had a great imagination and gave me a B-plus for effort."

"Well done! You'll go on to write your own bestiary someday, you'll see." The dragon smiled and returned to tuning the piano.

"So," Kenny said as he emptied out his book bag, "what are we reading next?" A dozen different books gathered from his bedroom bookshelf fell out onto the grass.

For the next couple of weeks, the dragon and Kenny read every book that he owned.

"I had no idea the entire planet was populated by giant lizards like myself. What a rollicking time that must have been!" Grahame said of a book on dinosaurs.

"Hmpf! This Beowulf fellow had a severe anger management problem," he sneered after he and Kenny read the epic poem about the Nordic warrior. "He's quite a blackguard, if you ask me."

"You mean to tell me that these little creepy-crawlies turn into beautiful butterflies? Now *that's* true magic," he declared after studying Kenny's book on insects.

Some days the two were too excited to relax and read, so they would invent other fun activities to do.

"I had no idea you could make a kite out of stuff from around the house," Kenny said as they flew homemade kites on the hilltop one windy afternoon.

"Wow, I am no good with watercolors," the lad said with a sigh one dusky evening, "but this sunset sure is pretty. And your painting looks great!"

"My mom used to play a lot," Kenny said, sitting at

the piano stool. "She's gonna flip when she hears that I learned how to play 'Chopsticks.' It's her favorite."

One sunny Friday afternoon, the two were relaxing under the shade of the large willow. What made it extra comfy was that they were on an old rug Kenny's mom had brought up from the house for the dragon to sleep on.

"I'd love to hear more tales by these Grimm brothers," Grahame said, munching on a pear. "Their work is quite entertaining."

"I really like them too," Kenny agreed, grabbing a pear of his own out of the bushel basket. "You know, George, who owns the bookshop in town, said they didn't really create these stories."

"Really? Who did?"

"The locals in the countryside. They told their stories to the brothers, who just collected them and wrote them down," Kenny answered.

"Wow!" Grahame said with his mouth full of pear. "What a great town they must've lived in. Look at all the tales that came from it."

"Yeah. Too bad nobody in this town is like

that. Everybody here is more worried about their crops than telling stories," said Kenny, looking down at Roundbrook from the hilltop.

"I can understand that. We all need food," Grahame said, picking his teeth. "But I bet you could come up with a grand tale of your own. And I could help you write it."

"Really?" the boy said, looking up.

"Sure. Why not? Who else is going to create the next great stories for kids to read?" the drake replied.

Kenny thought about this for a moment, then looked down at the books scattered around him on the blanket. "Grahame," he said, "a lot of the other kids in town . . . they don't . . . well . . . they don't really get me. I don't even know if they like me."

"Nonsense. Complete nonsense," the dragon declared, then began counting off on his clawed fingers. "You're well read, you love nature, you love food, music, art, poetry . . . what's not to like?"

The boy sighed. "I just wanted to say," he said, still looking down, "you're the best friend I've ever had."

"Really?" Grahame replied. His lemony eyes were wide and glowing in the shade of the willow tree.

"You know, little bantling, you're all right in my book."

"Even though I have vicious coils?" Kenny said with a smile.

"Even with your vicious coils, you devil scourge!" said Grahame, and threw a pear core at Kenny—which he dodged with ease as he scuttled behind the trunk of the willow. "So tell me, are there any other storytellers like these Grimm brothers?"

"Oh, yes. George told me about another guy named Hans something." Kenny reappeared on the opposite side of the tree trunk. "I can get his book next." He lobbed a pear core of his own back at Grahame, which the drake caught in his toothy maw and spit back at the boy. Ducking as it flew overhead, Kenny added, "I should probably go see George tomorrow. I usually visit him once a week, and I haven't been to town in a while."

And so, early the next day, after his chores were finished, Kenny rode into town to return the borrowed books to his friend George.

It was on Main Street in the center of his

little town of Roundbrook that Kenny spied quite a gathering. Townsfolk and villagers were huddled around a newsboy, who was selling them the daily paper as fast as his little paws could go. The citizens mumbled, whispered, and growled amongst themselves.

*Grahame would enjoy a bit of local news*, Kenny thought as he hopped off his bike and wiggled into the mass.

"People will come from far an' wide. It will certainly create a ruckus, that's f'r sure," he overheard someone say.

"I don't believe it at all. This is rubbish!"

"No. I heard somebody saw it firsthand."

"But the children. I wonder if there should be a curfew?"

"Not to worry. The matter should be resolved very soon."

Then Kenny saw the headline:

DRAGON SPOTTED IN ROUNDBROOK!
INFAMOUS SCOURGE SEEN ON SHEPARD'S
HILL! FEAR NOT, CITIZENS—
EXTERMINATION IS IMMENENT!

WELCOME TO
INN

# *V. The Least Bit Worried*

KENNY STARED AT THE NEWSPAPER in disbelief. The town had found out about Grahame—and they wanted him "exterminated." What was Kenny going to do now?

"What if it ransacks our harvest? It would be devastating," an old farmer moaned.

"If that thing burns my crops, I'll get my revenge f'r sure," another sneered, clenching his fists.

"We could get a posse together and take him out! Who's with me?"

"Well, where is it?" someone else shouted.

The paperboy pointed to Kenny and said, "Ask

him. It's living on his hill, and he told our whole class about how he knew the dragon firsthand."

A hush fell over the group as they turned to look at the boy. A weird river-stone-in-the-stomach feeling hit Kenny hard, and the lad hopped on his bicycle and pedaled away as fast as he could.

Kenny skidded to a stop in front of George's store. The Burrow Bookshop was located on a quiet street with little storefronts lining both sides. Fortunately, it looked like no one from the gathering had followed him there.

A little bell tinkled as Kenny pushed the door open and slipped into the shop. As the oak door swung closed, he peered through the window one last time to see if he was being trailed—but there was no one to be seen on the cobblestone street outside.

As he exhaled and caught his breath, the familiar mixed scent of wood, old leather-bound books, and hot tea greeted him, and he made his way through the dusty labyrinth of dimly lit bookshelves and armchairs.

He approached the sales desk, which was cluttered with stacks of books, and peered over the countertop.

Charlotte, George's young shop assistant, poked her head out from the little office behind the counter. She was a bit older than Kenny, and quite popular around town. Her parents were tailors and lived right next door. She had been helping out at the shop for as long as Kenny could remember.

"Hey, Kenny, we haven't seen you in a while. How ya doing?"

"Hi, Charlotte. I'm okay, I guess." He plopped the borrowed books down onto the counter. "Have you seen George?" Lately, for some reason, Kenny felt a bit shy when he was around Charlotte. In fact, it was hard for him to look at her directly. She had such big, bright, sparkly eyes that he glanced at her just briefly, then had to look down at his feet.

"If you can believe it, he's actually gone out," she said with a chuckle. "He had to go down to the post office to sign for some mail. I think it might have been some official royal thingy from the palace."

Huh? Kenny had heard stories of George's past exploits during his service as a cavalier. For some reason, he couldn't picture his old friend doing the things he often recounted in his tales. He sometimes suspected that they were half-fabricated from all

the books the codger had read. But George was the smartest fellow in town as far as Kenny was concerned. If anyone would have answers on how best to handle the "Grahame situation," it would be him. Now, on the one day the boy needed him most, he was out.

"Hey! Did you see the paper today? A dragon! A *real live* dragon spotted near here. It's unbelievable!" Charlotte said as she took the books and sauntered down an aisle. "I heard Old Pops Possum saw it drinking from Parrish Creek."

*Great*, Kenny thought to himself. *Now everybody knows where Grahame is. It's just a matter of time before someone else spots him—probably frolicking about on the hilltop. What is taking George so long?* He hopped along, following Charlotte into the natural history section of the store. "Yeah, I know . . . crazy. Hey, can you let George know I'll stop back by tomorrow?"

"Are you sure you don't just want to hang out and wait? He'll probably be back soon, and I know he's been dying to see you," she said as she put the bestiary back up on the shelf.

"No," he replied as he glanced at the book.

"I got some stuff I need to take care of."

"Okay. You know the shop will be closed tomorrow, but he'll be home," Charlotte said, then stopped arranging the books. "Hey, Kenny, is everything all right?"

"I'm okay," he replied. "I just got a lot on my mind."

"With a wild monster on the loose, I can understand, but hey—don't worry," the lass said with a smile and those big, sparkly eyes, "I'm sure everything is going to be just fine."

Heading back up the hill, the boy found the dragon with a wreath on his head, reciting lines to a captive audience consisting of Kenny's parents and their flock of sheep (who had by now gotten used to Grahame's presence).

"Not for thy fairy kingdom. Fairies, away! We shall chide downright, if I longer stay." With this declaration, the dragon ran around the hilltop, causing the sheep to scatter in all directions. He stopped when he noticed Kenny walking his bike toward them.

"Hey there, bantling, you're just in time! You can play Oberon," he said with a toothy grin.

"Hullo," Kenny replied. He leaned his bike against the trunk of the large weeping willow and trudged over to his parents. He flopped down on the blanket next to them and upset a glass of lemonade.

"What is it, Kenneth? What's wrong?" His mom wiped his face with the bottom of her apron. He pulled away from her and reached into his satchel.

"This," he answered, and stood up, handing the newspaper to Grahame.

"What is it, Kit?" his father asked. "What's it say?"

"It says," Grahame read aloud, scanning the article, "that I am to be 'exterminated.'" Kenny's parents exchanged glances. "Look here, the daft scribe misspelled 'imminent.' Ha!" He continued reading the paper, flipping through the pages. "Ooo! Look here, word puzzles!"

"What! Aren't you the least bit worried?" asked Kenny.

"Not at all. There will be no exterminations—*imminent* or otherwise," Grahame replied with a wink. "Now come on. We're getting to the good part of the play."

"I'm not feeling very theatrical today. Can I just watch?"

"Sure. But I expect a bouquet at the end for my grand performance," the dragon said with a smile.

Kenny sat with his parents and continued watching Grahame. The drake carried on, seemingly oblivious to the ruckus that was brewing in town. Kenny's dad quietly relaxed, sipping some lemonade, while his mom knit a pot holder. And even though the boy appeared calm, that river-stone-stomach feeling had not gone away.

## *VI. Kerfuffle Down in Roundbrook*

LIKE A BULLDOZER, KENNY SHOVED his toys and books under his bed. His mom had told him to clean his room and drop off his dirty clothes before leaving for the day. The boy ran to the laundry room, leaving a trail of shirts and socks, and dumped his clothes in the hamper. All he could think about was speaking to George about Grahame.

Just after breakfast, Kenny found himself back in the center of town. This time, however, it seemed like there were even more people milling about, and certainly quite a few who were not local. It was difficult for the boy to even navigate his bicycle down the street, so he hopped off and walked through the throng, worried about what had brought them all out.

It didn't take long for him to find that his suspicions were correct.

There on the corner of Main Street, Old Pops Possum was describing his encounter with Grahame.

"It was as big as that building," he said, pointing at the Roundbrook Inn.

The crowd oohed.

"With glowing, fiendish eyes and teeth like blood-dripping daggers. I am sure it had killed and was washing the gory evidence away. I barely escaped with my life," he continued.

The crowd aahed.

Kenny bent his head low as he passed so that no one, especially Old Pops, would see him. "This can't be happening," he muttered to himself.

He turned the corner and ran smack-dab into a band of roving minstrels singing tales of terrible dragons, gallant knights, and beautiful maidens. As they moved gracefully past him, they were

followed by a large pack of children with wooden play-swords battling each other, yelling, "I slay you, dragon! I slay you!"

Watching in total shock as the kids ran down the street, Kenny bumped into a vendor pushing a large cart.

"Dragon-embroidered tunics and tees!" the stout fellow yelled. "Get your official shirt with the Roundbrook dragon on it!" He paused for a moment and looked down at Kenny. "You look like a small," he said, and dropped a shirt into the boy's hand. It was emblazoned with a cartoonish, goofy drake blasting orange fire. Kenny's eyes went wide. He threw the shirt to the ground and got back on his bike. He was in such a rush, he almost ran over a little girl biting the head off a dragon-shaped cookie.

Regaining his composure, he found his way to the quiet alley where George's shop was. He slid off his bicycle and pounded on the heavy wooden door. The sign in the smudged window read CLOSED ON SUNDAY.

An elderly gentleman badger, older than his father, answered. He had gray hair and a white beard and mustache, and he spoke in a gravelly yet spirited voice.

"Kenny, my lad! My squire! So very good to see you! Come in! Come in!" he said as he welcomed the boy into the shop, locking the door behind him. They walked behind the counter, through the office, up the stairs, and into his little home on the second floor. "Charlotte mentioned you had stopped by. Can I get you a drink? Birch beer, perhaps?"

"Um, sure," Kenny replied as he sat down in the study next to their ongoing chess game. The old fellow had taught the boy chess years ago, and from that day on, there was always a game going. "Because," George had once told him, "in life, you must always plan your moves. Think before you act. Move toward a favorable outcome." Right now Kenny couldn't think of chess strategies at all, or any sort of "favorable outcome" for Grahame, based on what he'd just seen in town.

He glanced around the cluttered, dusty room. An antique clock ticked in the corner beneath a faded tapestry hanging on the wall. A large chest with a huge padlock was sitting in the opposite corner. Kenny didn't recall having seen it before, but there were so many books stacked on every available surface that it had likely been buried during his past visits.

George walked in and sat down with two frothy mugs.

"Here you go, son, drink up! It's your turn, you know," the old fellow said as he gestured toward the game. "So sorry that I missed you yesterday.

I was beginning to wonder if you'd forgotten me. It certainly has been a while, and I've so much to tell you."

"Me too," Kenny replied, and took a sip of his birch beer.

"I am glad you returned the books you'd borrowed. I sold all our copies of *The King's Royal Bestiary* last night and had to order more. It seems like everyone is in a frenzy over this dragon sighting. But I can tell you it will be all over quite soon."

At this statement, Kenny's river-stone stomachache returned. But he had to remain calm and carefully explain to the old-timer about Grahame. If anyone could help his friend out of this mess, it would be George. He made his move on the chessboard. "Rook takes pawn."

"Bold move!" the codger exclaimed, and moved his knight forward. "So there's this exciting news I want to tell you about. . . ."

"Can I tell you first? Rook takes bishop."

"Of course, lad. Spit it out."

Kenny took a sip from his mug. "I made a new friend."

"A new friend, you say? From school? Have you been playing chess with him?" George chuckled. "Because you're certainly giving me quite a wallop on the battlefield today."

"Not from school, no. Actually, he's new in town. And I really want to introduce you to him. I think you guys will really get along."

"A friend of yours is a friend of mine. By all means, bring the lad by. In fact—"

There was a knock at the door. With a "hold-that-thought" gesture, George ran downstairs and answered it. Kenny couldn't see much from where he was sitting, but it sounded like someone was delivering a package. "A friend of yours is a friend of mine," he said to his mug, and smiled. Perhaps this wasn't going to be so difficult after all. The stomachache began to fade, and he heard a hearty "Thank you, sir!" from downstairs right before the door slammed shut.

George returned to his study holding a large, ornately sealed scroll. He was smiling from ear to ear. He sat down on the trunk with the large padlock.

"What?" Kenny said. "What is it?"

"Yesterday I received word from the royal

palace, officially requesting me to come out of retirement," George said, pointing to some letters on his desk.

So it was true. The old-timer really had worked for the king after all. His stories of life as a cavalier, an armored horseman, were real.

"And today," George said as held up the scroll, "I received my official orders for one final task. And it is a most honorable task, I might add."

"Orders?" Kenny asked. But the answer was slowly dawning on him. He glanced down at the trunk with the padlock. On a small, rusty brass plate it read FROM HIS MAJESTY'S ROYAL ARMORY. PROPERTY OF GEORGE E. BADGER.

King. Orders. Armor. George was a knight.

The old gent stood gallantly, opened the scroll, cleared his throat, and read:

**My Dear George,**

It has been ages since we last spoke. I do hope this letter finds you still in the best of health, and your little shop thriving. The court has never quite been the same since you retired.

If I may be so bold as to get right to the point, I would ask one last request requiring your special skills for our great land. It seems there is a bit of a kerfuffle down in Roundbrook that only you can resolve. I do hope you are up for it, as there is no one else in all our land who can handle this as well, and as professionally, as you. You're such a saint for doing this!

As always, I remain your faithful friend (and ruler),

The King

P.S. Don't let me down, I've bet 4 to 1 you'll be triumphant.

P.P.S. Can you send over a copy of the bestiary? I seem to have misplaced mine.

George stood with his hands on his hips, clearly invigorated by the letter. "Well, what do you think of that?"

The river-stone had expanded beyond Kenny's stomach. He could feel it pressing into his throat. He knew what George was going to say. But he had to ask. He needed to know for sure. "What is it that he is asking you to do?"

The knight opened the trunk, revealing

a complete suit of armor. It was elaborately engraved, yet tarnished in spots. "My dear boy," he said, pulling out a long, gleaming sword, "I am his devil-dispatcher. His scourge-remover. I am the kingdom's number one dragon-slayer."

## VII. *Imminent Extermination*

THE GOLD-HILTED SWORD SHIMMERED in the morning light as George swiped the air with the weapon. The knight went through a series of attack motions, then stopped, a bit winded, and grinned at Kenny.

The river-stone stomachache finally pushed the breath out of the boy. Dizzy and light-headed, he dropped his mug on the chessboard,

drowning the pieces in a fizzy, brown deluge. In a blink, George dropped the sword and caught Kenny as the lad was about to topple backward off his stool.

"Little squire!" he cried as he helped Kenny up. "Are you okay?"

The young rabbit caught his breath, and his eyes slowly focused on the kindly, brave face of George. This codger was certainly not at all what he expected. He was a knight, a royal guardsman, and a dragon-slayer.

And if the stories George had shared with him over the years were even half-true, then he had to warn Grahame.

Immediately.

"I've got to go," Kenny said as he headed for the door. The knight stopped him.

"But you just got here. Are you okay? Is it . . ." George paused, kneeling down to look the lad in the eyes. "Are you worried? About me? Because you don't have to be, son. Once I get suited up and on that hilltop, this monster will be slain in moments. I know how to handle these devils. You can even watch, or help, if your parents allow it."

It was too much for the lad. Kenny dashed out of the shop without even a good-bye. He pedaled as fast as his legs could go from the center of town. He mind was so full of worry that he didn't even notice that the crowd was now much larger than it had been previously. In fact, villagers were lining up on either side of the street.

George had been his hope—his only hope—

of figuring out what to do with the dragon. If there was *anyone* in the village, outside of his family, who would understand Grahame wasn't a threat, it would have been George. And now he was preparing to come up and slay his best friend. And with orders from the king himself, how could he not follow them?

Then his mind flashed to the newspaper headline and what the paperboy had said. Was this mess somehow all his fault? Had he verified Old Pops's story by declaring what a "real" dragon was like during his book report?

As he pedaled even faster, the gears in Kenny's mind clicked and whirred, trying to find a solution for his friend. "Perhaps Grahame could hide out in his cave for a little while until this blows over?" he said, thinking out loud. "I bet Mom and Dad would let him live in our barn if he had to . . . even though it is a little tight." He was almost to the top of Shepard's Hill now. "Grahame will know what to do," he said as he hopped off his bike.

He found the dragon examining himself in an old full-length mirror, rubbing something onto his skin with a tattered flannel shirt.

"Kenny! Have a look at this," he said with that familiar toothy grin. "Your mom gave me some floor wax that polishes my scales up nicely. Look at this sheen! It really brings out the iridescence in my complexion."

Kenny was panting, completely out of breath. "Grahame . . . you . . . have . . . to go. George is . . . coming . . . to fight you!"

"George is coming to what? Why? What's he upset with me for? I didn't damage one single page of his books. Okay, well, I did scorch the cover of that silly bestiary a little, but it totally had me in stitches. Honestly, I don't know where some writers get their crazy ideas from. A 'camelopard'? Of all the—"

"Grahame!" Kenny interrupted. "He's a knight. A dragon-slayer who works for the king!"

The drake hissed, looked at the young rabbit for a second, then resumed polishing his scales, though in a much more frenetic fashion. "I thought he was your *friend*. I thought we had a lot in common: a fellow book lover, a fellow connoisseur of the finer things in life. Not some courtly bane sent for my *imminent extermination.*" He threw the rag down on the ground, walked toward his cave entrance, and began tidying.

"He's not like that!" Kenny squeaked as he followed the dragon. Kindly old George had been his friend for as long as he could remember. "He's a good guy. He taught me how to play chess, and he introduced me to all these good books we've been enjoying." The dragon kept his back turned to the lad. Kenny's heart started beating faster and faster. "What are we going to do?" he asked.

"*I* am not going to do anything," the dragon replied in an icy tone. "As I told you before, that was the sport of all my brethren, not me. That's why I am still here today and they are all gone. Slain by knights like your 'good friend' George. You tell him there will be no battle between us. No bloody Roman holiday. I won't have it."

"He has orders from the king himself," Kenny pleaded, "and the whole town is gathering together for this—"

"King, schming!" Grahame turned to face the boy. His eyes were glowing and wisps of smoke were rising out of his nostrils. "What does he know? When was the last time *he* sat down and talked to a dragon? Instead the cadger sends some carking varlet up here to do the dirty deed—without even a 'Hello. How are ya today? Mind if I cut your throat?'"

Grahame calmed down, picked up his rag, and began polishing himself again. "Now, if George wants to come up for some ginger beer and a good game of chess, well then, I'd be quite happy to see him and let his shady past stay where it belongs. But no weapons or pointy things that he can stick, hurl, or jab me with."

Kenny slumped his shoulders and looked down. "I'm afraid it's not going to happen that way."

"Little bantling," said Grahame with a sigh as he stopped admiring himself in the mirror. He bent low enough to look Kenny right in the eyes. "Don't worry. I just know *you* will think of something to make this right. Come on now, you're the well-read, smart one, remember?"

Flabbergasted, Kenny said nothing. The dragon resumed polishing his scales and admiring himself in the mirror as if he was without a care in the world. His mind whirling, Kenny grabbed his bicycle and left.

Normally the arduous ride up Shepard's Hill meant a fast-paced, exciting ride down. But the boy simply walked his bike back toward home. The high-noon sun had warmed the soft ground, and there was a gentle, lazy breeze whispering through the leaves as he made his way down the hill. Dragonflies and butterflies flitted all about; one even alighted on his handlebars, but Kenny didn't notice any of this.

"What on earth am I going to do?" he said to himself. Both of his best friends were to be pitted against each other in a battle to the death. Who would win? Would Grahame just lie there, refusing to fight, and be slaughtered? Or would George—much older now than he was back in his heyday—be burnt to a crisp? The river-stone feeling had taken over his entire body, and he swallowed hard to hold back the river itself that welled up in his eyes. Parking his bike on the porch, he was startled by his father bursting out of the front door.

"Kit! Hurry, boy, you're just in time!" his

dad exclaimed. His mother strolled out of the house behind him, tying a kerchief around her head.

"W-what's going on? Where are we going?" Kenny replied. For a moment, his parents' excitement distracted him from the heavy responsibility he was feeling.

"There's a parade in town! We just got word," his mom answered as she hopped aboard their sheep-drawn cart. "It's supposed to be quite a procession. Your father hasn't been this excited since . . . since . . ."

". . . you made that apple-crumble pie for my birthday! Now come on, son!" his dad said, slapping the spot right next to him on the driver's bench. "I'll even let you drive!"

"You don't understand," Kenny said. "Why do you think they're even having a parade?"

Both his parents blinked and looked at each another.

"An early celebration of the annual Corncob Festival?" his mom guessed, though it sounded more like she was asking the question.

"Pig wrestling?" his dad added, also in an "I'm-

not-so-sure-is-this-a-trick-question" sort of way.

"You guys haven't been in town for a while," said Kenny. "This is all about Grahame. I'm sure of it."

"Really?" his father replied. "I don't know 'bout that." And he paused for moment, mulling it over. "What would the parade be for?"

"Why don't we go into town and see for ourselves?" his mother suggested.

Kenny sighed and slowly climbed up onto the cart with his parents. It seemed that as much as he might try to escape it, he found himself heading right back into Roundbrook, and right back into his worst fears.

## *VIII. George Our Slayer*

SO IT TURNS OUT THAT GEORGE really was a royal knight. I suppose that truly does make this a fairy tale, for one cannot conjure up an image of dragons without thinking of brave knights and impudent kings. These days, however, there are not too many stories of this sort left. And many involve much darkness before their happy ending, so we must march on and see what is in store for our little lad, Kenny.

Kenny squinted at George, who shone from head to toe in golden fluted armor. He was astride his brilliant white mount, which was adorned in rich fabrics and tassels. In one gauntleted hand, he carried a large shield with a fierce dragon etched into it. In the other, he held a long lance with a faded royal standard hanging from its pointed tip.

People had turned out from all over—some had even traveled in from as far as Meadow Falls. The streets were jammed with zealous townsfolk yelling and waving brightly colored banners with the word GEORGE printed on one side and DRAGON-SLAYER on the other. From the rooftops, revelers threw flower petals down to the gallant knight below. Ladies swooned, and trumpets and horns blared as the procession began its march down the cobblestone streets.

"George our slayer! George our saint!" the chant from the crowd rang out through the air.

Kenny felt dizzy. His mother and father were confused. "Wait a second, why the heck is the bookshop owner all gussied up on a steed?" his

father asked aloud. An urchin standing next to them, waving a wooden sword, smiled and said, "That old-timer there is Georgie, the knight who's gonna go up on that hill tomorrow an' kill the vicious dragon."

Kenny's father's eyes went wide. His mother put her paw to her mouth. "Oh my!" she cried. Both of them looked over to their son. He was completely deflated. How could this be stopped?

Kenny's father knelt down in front of him. "Kit, you were right. You've got to get to your pal George and tell him what's going on. Ma and I will go back and talk to Grahame."

"It's useless," Kenny said over the din of the cheering crowd. "I've already tried speaking to Grahame, but he doesn't understand." The river from his stomach started burning in his eyes again.

His mom put her hand on his shoulder. "We'll be sure to discuss it with him over lunch. You know that a full stomach allows the brain to be hungry for common sense. We'll talk to him."

They turned to go. "You gotta make this right with George, son," his father said. "I know you can do it."

Kenny watched his parents shuffle off into the sea of rowdy, screaming villagers. His mother gave one quick glance over her shoulder and nodded before they disappeared into the mass. He stood there, dazed, as the bystanders pushed and shoved their way around him, following the parade. "It's no use trying to get close to George," he muttered to himself. "And even if I could, he won't be able to hear me. I'm just going to have to wait this out."

And so he did. Kenny sat all afternoon and watched as the boisterous gathering cheered and led the proud, chivalrous knight clear across town and back again. As his eyes followed George trotting about on his gallant mount, Kenny thought to himself, *Maybe I overreacted back at the shop. Maybe I should have stayed and talked to George. After all, we are good friends too. It shouldn't be so hard to tell him about Grahame.* The procession finally stopped at the center of town, at the old Roundbrook Inn, where they poured into the tavern to continue the celebration.

Kenny ran into the crowd, wiggling his way through the legs and butts, and peered in through a greasy window. There was George, standing on the bar and toasting, with the townsfolk pressed all around him.

"He'll burn my crops for sure, you must get rid of him," one farmer yelled out.

"He'll sneak into our house and eat all three of my daughters," another woman cried.

"He'll destroy our homes!"

"Eat our livestock!"

"You HAVE to save us!"

"KILL THE DRAGON! KILL THE DRAGON!" they all began to chant.

"How can they want someone killed they don't even know?" Kenny said under his breath. "How can George just blindly do whatever the king says?" The river-stone stomachache was starting to melt away to another feeling—a fiery feeling.

"Good people of Roundbrook," George declared. "Fear not, for you will all be safe and sound—you have my word. Now go on home to your friends, your farms, your families, and rest easy. For when the sun sets tomorrow night, this *monster*, this *devil*, this *beastly scourge*, will be smitten from your land!"

Well, of course, the crowd burst into uproarious applause as they carried the knight out of the inn on their shoulders. Bidding them all good night, George took his weapons, hopped onto his steed, and headed back home. The shadows grew long, signaling the end of a busy day, as the knight turned down his empty street. There he found our lad Kenny, sitting and waiting on his doorstep.

"Kenny, my boy! My squire! You scooted off this morning so quickly. Where on earth did you go? Are you feeling better?"

Kenny took George's shield and lance from him while the knight dismounted. Immediately the lad was reminded of the night that he first met Grahame. They were bidding each other farewell as the drake handed back Kenny's own makeshift weapons. Now, as he held the *actual* weapons, he felt like the river within him was frozen. He shook it off, focusing on George, and replied, "A little bit. Actually, I came back to talk to you and—"

"Did you see the parade? I kept an eye out for you. What a sight! What a spectacle it was! I felt like I was in the prime of my youth once again!"

"I did," Kenny said, tying George's mount to a street sign. "I had just gotten back from seeing that friend of mine I was telling you about earlier. Remember? And I—"

"Can you help me with these buckles, lad?" George asked as he rushed into his shop. He poked his head back out the front door when he realized that Kenny hadn't moved. "Come on! I do want to hear about your friend, but I have to tell you about tomorrow! Just give me a hand with this coat of mail." Kenny sighed, trailing behind him, arriving back in George's little home on the second floor. "That's a good boy. I've . . . umf . . . forgotten . . . how hot this armor is. I haven't worn it in years!" the knight said as he began to unbuckle the metallic pieces.

Kenny helped his friend out of his suit of armor and set the parts carefully back into the trunk. Even though the pieces were heavy and clanged while George wriggled out of them, Kenny had never seen his old pal so sprightly before.

"Phew! That's much better," the knight said,

and went to the icebox. "I'm parched—do you want something to drink?" Kenny went to answer, but before he could speak, the excited George handed him a bottle of birch beer and cut him off. "Hold on a sec, I'll be right back. I've so much to talk to you about, and I need my . . ."

The lad heard George's voice drift away as the knight scurried back downstairs to the bookshop for something.

He had to tell George about Grahame. He took a big swig from his birch beer. "Just take a deep breath and say it," he said to himself. "George, the dragon you are about to slay is more interested in buttercups than battles. So you have to call off the fight. Okay? Okay."

While he waited for the knight's return, the lad looked around the transformed study, where the ongoing chess game had been. On top of the chessboard lay the scroll with the "official orders" from the king. Above a stack of books, on George's wall, hung the dusty, faded tapestry. Kenny approached it and, after blowing off a layer of dust, could now see that it was embroidered with a knight piercing a dragon in the heart.

Finally his eyes fell on the polished shield with the dragon etched on it. The image was beastly: The wicked drake had fire blasting from its mouth and nose. It was nothing at all like Grahame, who just the other night had used his fire breath to light his dad's pipe by blowing a tiny spark out of his left nostril. However, like Kenny's frying pan from his first visit with the dragon, George's shield was blotched with scorch marks . . . *real* scorch marks made from fiery breath.

George dashed back into the study. "I knew

this was here somewhere, I just had to dig around a bit." He cleared his table of the chessboard and the scroll and slapped down a large brown roll of parchment.

"It's a map of the area," he said, beaming, "and *I* would like to discuss strategy with *you*, Kenny. You know Shepard's Hill like the back of your paw, so how do you think we should best make our approach?"

George sat, eagerly awaiting the lad's response. Kenny had never seen him so vibrant, so alive, before. This wasn't going to be easy to do, but he had to do it. "Um . . . I can't help you, George," he said.

*There*, he thought to himself. *That wasn't so hard. Keep going.*

"You see," he continued aloud, "there is, um . . . something very important I've been meaning to tell you about the dragon."

Sensing that something was once again amiss, the knight put his large arm around the young rabbit and spoke softly. "Spit it out, lad. What is it? What's troubling you? Are you afraid of it?"

"Not really," Kenny replied, furrowing his brow a bit.

"Because it's okay if you are," said George.

"No. Really, I'm not," Kenny said, setting his bottle down, that fiery feeling flickering in his stomach. "You see—"

"You are so brave, young squire. Charlotte told me it was sighted very close to your house, and I know you're family's in danger—"

"NO!" Kenny yelled. The fire in his stomach completely overtook him, burning away the river-stones. "That's not it at all! Just listen to me! You don't understand anything! Grahame is a good dragon—a peaceful dragon. He doesn't like to fight. He's never fought a day in his life, but his brothers did, and they were all killed by knights. *Knights just like you*, and now you have orders from the king to kill him, and the stupid king doesn't even know him! *You* don't even know him. Do you know what he likes to do?"

George was blinking at the boy. His mouth was slightly open.

"He likes painting sunsets, listening to classical music, playing piano, reading, and crème brûlée. He's . . . he's . . ." The boy could no longer keep the river down, and it started trickling out, burning his eyes. "He's my best friend. And I don't want to lose either of you in some dumb fight to the death."

With his mouth still agape, George studied the boy, watching him wipe his eyes with the sleeve of his shirt. Sniffling, Kenny got up to leave and turned back to the old man. "You said 'a friend of yours is a friend of mine.' Of all the people in the world who could have helped me and Grahame, I thought of you. You two are the only ones who really understand me." Kenny stood in the doorway, looking the old knight in the eyes. "I even thought you two might just become friends." With that, the boy ran down the stairs, out the front door, and into the gaslit streets toward home.

# *IX. A Well-Willed Chap*

As Kenny bolted off the main street in Roundbrook, he knocked over a cart of dragon trinkets, and they spilled near a group of townsfolk who were sharing a keg of ale and laughing loudly. As he scurried past them, he heard one exclaim, "I bet seven to one that the dragon flambés the old coot in five minutes. It's gonna be a *roasting* good time!"

"I can't wait," another added. "It'll be a *hot* time up on the hill tomorrow. A *scorcher* for sure!"

A boy sitting with the group spied Kenny and ran into the alley, blocking his way.

"Hey, you live up on that farm near the hill, doncha?" he asked. "I heard you seen that dragon up there. Didja? Maybe eatin' a cow or somethin'?"

Kenny had seen this prickly kid before in school. He was a couple of years older and a couple of pounds heavier, hence his nickname, "Porky."

"Yeah," he said, looking Porky in the eyes. That fiery feeling was still in his stomach. "I've seen the dragon. And there isn't gonna be a fight tomorrow.

So forget about it." Kenny's heart was pounding. He waited for the wallop to come from the young ruffian.

"Now don't worry yer little head," Porky's father said. He put his burly hand on Kenny's shoulder reassuringly and slowly separated the two boys. "If ol' Georgie can't get that beast, well then, we'll all go up there and kill 'im—right, boys?"

Amidst the whooping of the revelers, Kenny wiggled free and took off as fast as his legs would take him, leaving Roundbrook far behind.

It was almost sunset by the time Kenny arrived back at his little farmhouse. His father was bringing the sheep in from the fields, and he could smell the aroma of vegetable stew as he approached his front porch. A cool breeze welcomed him home amidst a trio of chirping crickets.

Kenny slumped through the house and flopped down on his bed. He pushed all his pillows off the covers and got under his blanket, staring at the cracked, patched ceiling.

*Why couldn't this be like a fairy tale? Why did the dragon*

*have to show up and be a* good *dragon? Why did the only person in town who just happened to be a dragon-slayer also happen to be my only other friend in the world?*

He looked down at his bookshelf and gazed at the books that George had given him over the years. In some of them, there were wizards and witches who could give you enchanted weapons or supernatural powers that allowed you to overcome your foes and save the day. Kenny's life didn't have these villains intent on doing nothing but bad things—it was more complicated than that. Come to think of it, he had no foes, really, except now maybe all the townsfolk who had come to witness this battle.

*Sure,* he thought, *this could be the most famous battle of all time. Folks have heard about something this big, but they've never seen anything like it—but these are my friends. And they're betting on who will win!*

"Kenneth"—his mother interrupted his thoughts—"I've invited someone for dinner who really wants to see you."

Kenny pulled his ears over his eyes and rolled

over in his bed. "I don't want to come out, Mom. I just want to stay in here."

"I think you should get up, son," his mom said as she entered his room and put his folded laundry in his dresser. She sat down on the bed and stroked

his furry head. "I just made you a bowl of my vegetable stew, and there are fresh butter rolls for dipping."

"Is there ginger beer?" Kenny asked, peeking out from under his ear.

"No," his mother answered as she rose and went to the door. "But your friend has brought you some birch beer. So wash up and come on out for dinner."

Kenny washed his hands and face and peered into the kitchen. Sitting at the table with his mom and dad was George.

"Hello," the boy said, plopping down in his chair and staring at his stew.

"Hello, Kenny," said George. "I hope you don't mind me following you back home. I wanted to talk to you about tomorrow. Your parents tell me that the dragon is quite a well-willed chap, and—"

"Grahame," Kenny interrupted. "His name is Grahame."

"Er, uh . . . well, perhaps this Grahame and I can have a chat about tomorrow and see to a . . . uh, is that Grahame like the cracker?"

"Indeedy it is," Kenny's father said through a mouthful of butter roll. "But with an 'e' on the end."

"Oh. Ah, those are good," George said as if he was savoring the thought of them. Kenny looked at him for a moment, and then stared down at his stew, but he wasn't feeling hungry. He wondered if the codger ever felt the river-stones in his stomach. It almost seemed like the knight was having a harder time talking here at the dinner table than anything else. It was odd to think this was the same George who'd been so gallant, so chivalrous, earlier this afternoon astride his proud mount. And the same George he had known all these years, who had never left his bookshop.

"Anyways," George continued, "if this friend of yours is as good a spirit as you've said, well then, perhaps we can converse about the upcoming event and sort something out. What do you say?"

Kenny looked up from his soup bowl. George wasn't just some weapon for the king to wield whenever he wanted, after all. Whatever anyone had expected of him tomorrow, the knight was here with Kenny, willing to make amends. "Really?" he said. "You'd do that?"

"Certainly," George replied with a smile. "A friend of yours is a friend of mine—remember?"

"Good! I'm glad that's settled," said Kenny's mother, "'cause I've already invited Grahame for dessert and coffee. He should be here any minute."

Kenny looked up and smiled at his mother, then his father and George. All three were smiling back. Through the window, over their shoulder, he could see the familiar round shape of the dragon bounding across the twilight field toward their house. He took a deep breath, swallowed the stone in his throat, and hoped that dessert would go as well as dinner had.

# *X. A Dragon and His Wrath*

"I BROUGHT SOME NEW POEMS TO RECITE over dessert. Is it crème brûlée again tonight?" Grahame asked as he pushed his large head through the window to hover next to the dinner table. He smiled his toothy grin when he saw Kenny, then noticed the old fellow with the white beard and mustache sitting at the table. "Ho there, we've got some company. Mayhaps a fellow poet?"

"Kenneth, why don't you introduce your friend to Grahame?" his mom asked.

"Any friend of Kenny's is a friend of mine, as long as it isn't that daft knight sent to execute me," Grahame snorted. George fake-coughed a little.

"Um, actually, this *is* him," Kenny said. "Grahame, meet my old friend George. George, this is my new friend, Grahame."

Kenny bit his lip and held his breath. His father slurped his second helping of stew, while his mom quietly got up from the table to start washing the dishes. George and Grahame eyed each other for some time, waiting for the other to speak first and break the uncomfortable silence.

"So," George said at last, "I can say I haven't seen a dragon in many, many years. In some ways it's like seeing a familiar face."

"Yes. Well, get used to it," said the dragon in an icy tone. "This is one face that is not leaving the area anytime soon, either by hook or by crook. Are we clear on that, Beowulf?"

"Now, now," said George, rising. "There is no need for that kind of name-calling."

"What else should I call you? Enlighten me, *great savior*," the drake responded. Kenny could see a wisp of smoke wafting from Grahame's nostrils. He wondered if he should stand between the two of them to keep the peace, but he caught his father's eyes and was silently spoken to. (Of course, you know what I am talking about: when your mom, or dad, talks to you with nothing more than a look or glance and nary a word is said.) Kenny understood and remained in his chair, appearing calm, as his parents were clearly doing.

"Beowulf was a barbarian, an uncultivated lout! I am none of those things. I have been trained under the king himself in the proper manner for dragon removal, and I—"

"Agreed," Grahame said.

"A-a-agreed what?" stammered George. Kenny and his parents exchanged glances.

"I agree Beowulf was a barbarian. He couldn't just dispatch of Grendel, he had to swim down to his home and butcher his mother as well."

George blinked. "P-precisely." He looked at Kenny, who noticed the slightest curl of a smile hiding underneath his mustache. "Now, what he should have done was lock up that insolent ogre and have him do hard labor for his injustices."

"Interesting," Grahame said as he paused for

a moment and looked at Kenny. "Do you think a ruffian like that can truly be reformed?"

And there it was.

Kenny realized he had been holding his breath the entire time, and he finally let it out with great relief. He and his parents watched and listened as George and Grahame discussed *Beowulf* and whether Grendel could become an upstanding member of society. Things were going swimmingly by the time coffee was served, and the two reminisced about adventures they'd had in their youth. There were jokes and laughs afterward as the dragon brûléed the desserts (with a flicker of flame from his left nostril).

Everybody went out to the front porch so that Kenny's father and George could enjoy their after-dinner pipes.

"You know, Grahame, Kenny was right. You are wonderful company! I haven't had good dinner conversation like that in a dog's age," George said as he shook the dragon's large, scaly paw.

"Agreed. You really are a well-read good fellow," Grahame replied, lighting George's pipe for him. "I suppose we do have a lot in common."

He looked over at Kenny, "Well done, little bantling. Well done."

"Holy smokes! What's that?" Kenny's dad asked as he pointed with his pipe stem.

A line of bobbing lights was streaming from the center of Roundbrook toward Shepard's Hill. Everybody stared at the sight for some time.

"Well, well, well," George said with a sigh.

"Are those all night fishermen?" asked Grahame.

"Those are people getting ready for tomorrow," said Kenny. The river-stone feeling was back, and he wondered if they all felt it as well.

"Yep, son," his father replied, sucking on his pipe. "I believe you are correct."

"That's a mess of people," Kenny's mother added, knitting nervously. "And they are coming with a lot of expectations. You boys are not going to be able to get out of this easily."

Kenny watched the procession cross the bridge over Parrish Creek and down the road toward Shepard's Hill. He swallowed down the river-stones and allowed the gears in his head to click and whir. He thought of what George had taught him about planning ahead for his moves in chess. He had just gotten his two friends to see eye to eye, but how was he going to do the same with an entire town?

His father creaked back in his rocker. "I heard people were bettin' on who was gonna come out on top of this ruckus. Sorry, George, but a lot them was bettin' odds against ya."

George chuckled as he drew a long puff off his pipe. He sighed. "Well, I guess I shouldn't be surprised. What can you expect from an old retired shopkeeper? And you know what they say: Come not between a dragon and his wrath."

"Heh, that's from *King Lear*," Grahame said, watching the bobbing lanterns gathering around the bottom of the hill, "one of my favorite performances from Shakespeare. I wonder if *he* ever met a dragon? He'd certainly know what to do with a crowd like this."

And the gears in Kenny's brain finally all clicked into place. "That's it!" Kenny squealed, causing everybody to jump. "I know what we have to do, and we don't have much time to do it! Everyone inside!"

## *XI. Rolling Out a Purple Carpet*

THE FIRST PART OF THE BOY'S PLAN was keeping the spectators off the hill. And it wasn't going to be easy. As Kenny and his father approached the anxious gathering, they realized the group was looking to stake out prime seats for tomorrow's battle. There were so many townsfolk present, they seemed like they were everywhere, illuminating the entire hillside with their lanterns and torches. Kenny stopped just short of the crowd. "I—I dunno if this is going to work." His father knelt down, put his hand on the boy's shoulder, and looked his son in the eyes.

"Don't you worry, Kit," he said. "If there is one thing I know how to do, it's herdin' sheep."

He held up his lantern and addressed the crowd. "Ho there, what's all this about?"

"We're here to see the dragon-slaying tomorrow," someone shouted out.

"Ain't no devil-dragon on my land," Kenny's father replied, pulling up a stalk of grass and putting it in his mouth, "so you all best head on."

"Yer dead wrong, farmer Rabbit," a gruff voice said. The crowd parted and a burly fellow, Porky's father, stepped up. "Old Pops Possum seen 'im here the other day drinkin' in the creek."

"Old Pops told me he pulled a catfish out of that creek the size of my prized ewe. If you ask me, I think he's the one drinkin' at the creek," he replied. The crowd laughed. Porky's father did not.

"Well, yer boy said he's seen this thing before. Told all the kids in school about it." He pointed at Kenny. "What do you say to that?"

Kenny's father turned and looked toward his son, "Kenneth, what's this all about? You know somethin' about dragons that you ain't telling me?"

This was Kenny's cue.

"Yes, sir. I was reading that *King's Royal Bestiary* about all the monsters. It said that though dragons are cold-blooded, they usually hunt at night. It also mentioned that they are often attracted to a bright light, like a moth—*an enormous, flying, bloodthirsty, fire-breathing moth.*"

That did it. The crowd began murmuring amongst themselves.

"Best to stay in tonight," he heard one fellow say.

"It is getting late," he heard another one add.

"Perhaps we should douse these lanterns," someone said from the back of the group.

Kenny's father eyed Porky's prickly dad for some time, calmly chewing on his grass stalk. Finally the rabble-rouser broke the stare and announced, "All right. Let's head back to town." He put his hand on his son's shoulder, and both turned to go. "We'll meet up here tomorrow at dawn. And then"—he looked back at Kenny—"ain't nobody gonna stop us from seein' this showdown."

Kenny exhaled as he and his father turned back toward the farm. "You see, son," his dad said, putting his arm around Kenny's shoulders, "there is always a pecking order. You find out who the leader is, spook him into goin' where you want him to, and the rest of the flock will follow."

Kenny looked up at his dad as they walked back home. In the warm lantern light, he seemed wise now, like Arthur's Merlin. And Kenny realized that his father's wisdom was gained from real experiences and not something he had read about in a book.

They both returned to a very busy household. Everyone was running around, including Charlotte, who had received word from George and arrived to help. Kenny smiled at her as she looked up from her sewing machine. "Hiya, Kenny! Heard about your plan," she said. "This is gonna be awesome!"

The boy felt his cheeks go warm and looked down at his feet. "I'd better check on Grahame," he said, and went out to the barn. The dragon was sitting with George, viewing the map of the hill by candlelight. The two were engaged in a very animated conversation, and Kenny's tin soldiers, building blocks, and a toy dinosaur were scattered about on the faded scroll.

It was agreed that Grahame should stay

in the barn until midnight so that no curious townsfolk would spy him. Secrecy was of the utmost importance, and they had one night only to prepare for tomorrow's big event.

A cool, foggy mist topped Shepard's Hill just before daybreak on the morning of the big battle. As the sun slowly rose in the pinkish sky, it burned away the fog just as the first spectators arrived. Porky's dad, of course, was leading the group, followed by Old Pops Possum.

"Holy smokes," Old Pops said with a whistle, "somethin' done happened to the landscape. That dragon's changed it all up."

And he was right, for the hilltop had been miraculously transformed. The enormous rocks from the side of the hill had all been moved—arranged on the grassy meadow to form the seats of an amphitheater. The seating surrounded an outdoor arena, with the dragon's cave rising up from the center. A faint smell of smoke was in the air, and Porky's dad was sure it was coming from the cave, but he could not see inside.

For you see, now there were large, richly woven, tattered tapestries covering the entrance to Grahame's lair. The enormous oaks and willow trees that flanked the sides were covered with a variety of lanterns and lights—which hung from nearly every bough and branch. The dragon's old upright piano, freshly painted in gold and black lacquer, was nestled underneath a willow covered in half-melted candles.

By lunchtime, the area was filling up at a quicker pace. Vendors had arrived and were selling all sorts of food and ale. Others sold tunics, toys, and pennants, just like the ones Kenny had seen in town. Children ran around the stony seats and grassy aisles playing knights and dragons. More than once, Kenny overheard wagers being made on who would come out victorious.

Late afternoon brought a surprise no one in town had expected. By now, most everyone from Roundbrook was present, and clearly word had spread to the neighboring villages, for there were far more sightseers than there were seats—leaving some to find viewing elsewhere. All were curious about the large, stately procession that was coming from the east road and heading straight up the hill. One vendor, standing on top of his cart, used his opera glasses to get a better look and cried, "The king! The king is coming!" A large group of onlookers rushed over to get a better view.

Sure enough, it was the king himself, arriving in a beautifully ornate horse-drawn carriage. Armed soldiers, who looked like younger versions of George, marched both in front of and behind him. They stopped at the back of the amphitheater and began constructing a small tower with box seats for His Majesty and his courtiers. From a hiding place high in the branches of a tree, Kenny watched the royal servants assemble the tower, finally rolling out a purple carpet for the king to walk upon.

The guards flanked both sides of the walkway, preventing any onlookers from getting too close to His Majesty. The king was followed by his two sons, a jester, and George—dressed in his finest clothing. With all eyes watching the king enter the royal box, Kenny hopped down from his hiding spot and scurried back down the hill. *This is just like a giant chess game*, he thought to himself. *Now I just have to move toward a favorable outcome.*

As the afternoon began to fade into evening, the waiting crowd began to grow restless. The rowdy bunch chanted and stomped their feet in unison. Few of them noticed little Kenny as he lit the lanterns. He knew this was it: It was time to finally set his plan into full motion. Setting alight the last lantern, Kenny looked down at his mother and gave her a nod. She solemnly walked up to the piano, lit the candles, and began playing an ominous melody. Immediately the entire gathering hushed to a breathy silence and looked toward the arena.

Kenny walked slowly to the center of the battlefield. He looked up in total awe—he had never seen this many people gathered together in his entire life. Strangely, the river-stone feeling was not present. Instead, he felt a fiery flicker of a feeling—something that cavorted about his insides. This was not a book report. There would be no grade handed to him at the end of this. Either his plan would work, or . . . one of his friends might not see the sun set that day. But they all trusted him: his mom, his dad, George, Grahame, and even Charlotte. They thought his plan was ingenious, and now it was all up to him.

He looked down at his two little paws, took a deep breath, and slowly opened a large, leather-bound book. He began to read in a shaky voice:

"*Draco*, Latin for 'dragon' and derived from the Greek word 'draconta,' is the biggest of all living creatures on Earth."

At this, murmurs and hushes were heard throughout the audience. Kenny continued, the fiery feeling danced throughout his chest and heart. "When the dragon comes out of its cave, it is often carried into the sky, borne into the air surrounded by blazes, for indeed it is rising up from the lower regions of Hades."

Audible gasps could be heard at this point. One mother put her paws over her child's ears.

The fiery feeling rushed up into Kenny's throat. He continued loud and clear so that nobody could miss a single word he said. "A dragon's strength is found within its long and dangerous tail. Tying the tail in a knot will render the foul beast harmless. But be warned, all drakes kill anything they catch with their vicious coils."

Kenny slammed the book shut, and the crowd jumped back in their seats. He asked aloud, with the fiery feeling dancing on his tongue, "Who among us shall vanquish this menacing scourge from our land?"

"I shall!" announced George in a clear voice. Everyone turned toward the royal box and watched him stride down the aisle, escorted by beautiful Charlotte. She was draped in elegant, ornate white robes with ribbons and flowers wrapped around her head. The knight was adorned in his golden armor, which had been polished to a mirrorlike shine. He held his decorated shield in one hand, Charlotte's arm in the other, and a crimson silken cape billowed and danced about behind them both as they walked toward the battlefield.

"First a kiss from a maiden fair," George proclaimed, "for this may be my final day upon the battlefield." Charlotte hugged the old man and pecked him on the cheek.

Seeing this, the tips of Kenny's ears grew warm. He shook off the feeling and continued,

"Great knight, not only will you need a courageous heart and beloved spirit to dispatch this beast, but you will also need magically enchanted weapons. Say now, have you these instruments of carnage?"

"I do," replied George, displaying his sword and shield for all to see. "But alas"—he looked down glumly—"they are not enchanted."

"Then they will not work. And death will most certainly greet you on the battlefield today!" Kenny declared. The audience rumbled with anticipation.

"Unless," he said in an "I-just-got-an-idea" tone, "unless there is a wizard, a mage here among us who can enchant your weapons." He gestured toward the crowd. "Is there anyone present who can perform such a supernatural task?"

Heads turned this way and that as the assembly of spectators looked to one another. Porky's dad yelled out, "Get on with it!" but he was immediately hushed.

Kenny took in a deep breath as he stood facing the hundreds of onlookers. "Come on," he whispered under his breath, "let's go."

And then someone stood up in the back of the

gathering near the king's tower and shouted, "Ho there!" Whispers murmured through the crowd and everyone craned their necks to see who it was.

An elderly figure, wearing a low brimmed hat and dressed in dark robes embroidered with strange symbols and stars, leaned on an old pitchfork as he rose. "I can enchantify yer weapons, if that is what you'd like," he said in a gravelly voice. The crowd parted as the mysterious character hobbled down to join Kenny and his companions at the center of the arena.

He walked up to George and announced, "Put yer sword away! It will do you no good. Instead, use this enchantificated pitchfork." He rubbed the mud and dirt off of the fork, revealing shimmering golden tines. He held the pitchfork high so that all in the audience could see.

"Pin the dragon's tail to the ground," he continued, "so that you may tie it in a knot and defeat the beast." The wizard then pulled a bottle from his robes and poured the liquid contents onto the knight's shield. "This will protect you from the monster's fiery breath. Now"—he paused, looking out to the audience—"now yer ready!"

The mass of viewers burst into applause as the old wizard hobbled through them back toward his seat. As they congratulated and patted the mage with cheers of praise, Kenny could feel his heart begin to race. "So it is done!" he declared, and all heads turned back to focus on the little buck. "Then there is only one thing that remains."

"There is?" George replied in a puzzled tone.

"You need bait to lure the drake from his smoky den," Kenny answered. The fiery feeling was strong now—it leaped out of his mouth and onto his shoulders.

"Is my royal challenge not enough to bring the beast out of hiding?" George asked.

"No. It will not do," answered Kenny. He was controlling not just his fiery anxiety, but the entire crowd as well. He pointed to Charlotte. "But she will!"

The audience gasped.

"Brave knight, there is but one thing a dragon finds irresistible: the sweet taste of a maiden fair. Bind this girl to the tree, and her screams for help will surely lure the beast from his devil-den!"

"No! No!" some voices in the audience cried, but most were shocked into stupefied silence.

George grabbed Charlotte by the wrists and tied her to the gnarled oak closest to the cave's entrance. At this, the unsettled crowd gasped and moaned louder than before, but the din could not block out Charlotte's pleas for help as she tried to free herself from her binds. Ignoring Charlotte's sobs, George threw off his cape and readied his weapons. Kenny stood at the entrance of the cave, spread out both hands, and cried, "THEN LET THE BATTLE BEGIN!"

# *XII. One Fierce Beast*

THE PIANO CONTINUED ON, NOW IN time with the weeping cries of Charlotte. Townsfolk began to get up and withdraw from the center arena. Some left the scene altogether.

"This is much more than I bargained for," Kenny heard one farmer cry out.

"Maybe this wasn't such a good idea," he heard another say.

"I—I—I don't need to see this," stammered a third.

As the handful of spectators headed up the aisles toward the exit, an enormous fireball erupted from the cave, instantly incinerating the tattered covers and billowing a cloud of hazy smoke out into the amphitheater. The thick, murky smog blanketed the attendees, who could now barely see one another, let alone anything else. The fleeing audience members froze with fright, not sure whether to run blindly off into the smoke or stay with the masses.

Then a cold, deep, reptilian voice thundered over the gathering. The sound seemed to be coming from everywhere. "Well, well, well. What a reception this is." Nobody made a peep, as all were trying to see any sign of the beast in the dense fog. A flapping noise began, and a warm, gusty wind blew the smoke away, revealing the large dragon *behind* the audience, next to the king's box seats, blocking any escape from the hilltop. Waving his enormous leathery wings, he smiled a jagged, toothy smile. "It looks like the whole town is here. Now this what I call a smorgasbord!" he roared.

Grahame inhaled deeply and blew a stream of fire straight up into the sky, causing glowing ash to rain down onto the amphitheater like fiery snow. He then leaped up on top of the king's tower and peered inside. "Arrah! Let's start with a royal appetizer!" he cackled.

"Back off! Go away! Shoo!" the king yelled as he grabbed his two sons and hid behind the jester.

"Dragon!" George's voice cut across the audience and snapped the beast's gaze from the king. "Your fight lies with me, ruffian!"

"Indeed it does," Grahame replied, and sprang from the tower, causing it to topple into pieces. He hovered over the crowd for a bit, his expansive beating wings sending trash, ash, and pennants swirling up into the air. The large drake then dropped down into the center aisle. This sent the audience screaming and running for their lives. The king clawed his way out of his wrecked tower. "My word, that is one fierce beast!" he said. "What do you think, boys?"

"Whoa!" they replied in unison.

"Devil! Prepare for your *imminent* extermination!" George yelled as he charged up the aisle toward Grahame.

"Little knight, I will eat you alive and use your *enchanted* weapon as my toothpick. Then I will dine upon this sweet maiden for dessert!" At this,

Grahame lunged over George, landing square in the center of the battlefield, and ramped about, thrashing his wings madly. The smoke billowed and rolled about in a very dramatic fashion—it wisped and whorled around Kenny's mom as she continued playing away on the piano.

"We have to flee, or he'll pick us off one by one!" Kenny heard someone yell.

"There's nowhere to run! We're fish in a barrel!" another responded.

Frozen in his front-row seat, Old Pops Possum fainted right on the spot. The young lad next to him waved his wooden sword and squealed, "Go, dragon!"

"Back off, you foul beast!" Charlotte yelled. Still bound to the tree, the feisty gal kicked at the dragon while George approached the arena slowly, pitchfork in hand like a lance. The knight's eyes remained fixed on Grahame, no matter where the dragon moved. George announced, "It's no use! This is your final hour!"

"We'll see about that," replied Grahame. He lashed his tail about and whipped the pitchfork right out of George's hand. It flew up in the air, plunging into the trunk of one of the oaks bordering the cave.

Grahame bellowed out a malicious laugh as he glimpsed the pitchfork lodged in the tree. With Grahame's attention diverted for the moment, George ran behind him and leaped upon his scaly back. He drew his sword and yelled, "Devil! Your end is nigh!"

At that the dragon bucked, like a wild horse, high into the air. Losing his grip, George dropped his sword, and it plunged into the top of the piano, creating a loud, dismal flat note. Kenny saw his mom pause for a moment and then continue playing more frenetically than ever. The knight held on for dear life as the beast vaulted about the battlefield in an effort to shake him off.

The audience members shrieked and hollered as they ran to and fro around the skirmish. However, some were so mesmerized by the action playing out in front of them that they edged in closer to better view the gritty battle, oblivious of the danger.

At last Grahame landed atop his cave, just over the entrance. Flexing his back muscles like a cat, he sent a ripple down his spine, loosening George's grasp. The dragon took full advantage of this opportunity and bucked again—this time sending the knight flying off his back. George was sent arcing over the battlefield, crashing into another tree. Branches snapped and cracked under the weight of the armor, as the beaten warrior was swallowed up by the thick foliage.

Once more Grahame laughed in a low, cold snicker. "You are finished, toy soldier. Now watch, all of you"—he turned toward the audience—"as I dine upon your delectable fair damsel!"

Most everyone in the crowd was silent, save for a few weak sobs. Kenny was wringing his hands and holding his breath. "It's almost over," he whispered to himself. "Come on, George."

Charlotte began screaming at the top of her lungs as the cackling dragon turned toward her. His back was now to the knight. George seized this moment and dropped down from the tree, pitchfork in hand, and pinned the drake's tail firmly into the ground. Kenny let out his breath.

"Back for more, are you? Enjoy your funeral pyre!" Grahame thundered. He inhaled deeply and exhaled in an effort to engulf the knight in a fiery ball of flames—but all that came out was a puff of smoke. He inhaled once again, but this time he gasped and coughed out only a smoke ring.

The crowd watched, completely stunned—there was George, holding the knotted tail in both hands. He untied Charlotte, pulled his sword from the piano, and announced, "The dragon has been defeated!" The audience cheered and applauded in a deafening roar. The knight looked over at Kenny, and the boy smiled.

But the cheering of the crowd turned into loud ranting as they clamored, "Off with his head! Off with his head!"

Kenny looked at George for some kind of sign, but the knight had positioned himself next to Grahame's head with his sword blade on the drake's blue, scaly neck. He gazed out toward the king. The crowd fell silent and turned in unison to look for the final command from their ruler.

The king stood up in front of the rubble that was once his tower and eyed the dragon as he

thoughtfully stroked his beard. Kenny watched one of his sons whisper something into the ruler's ear. The king turned to his boy and said, "What! I don't think so."

At this, the audience began murmuring amongst themselves. Kenny noticed that the second son was now whispering into his father's ear. The king turned to both of his sons and said, "All right. All right, if that is what you want."

Both sons smiled and nodded vigorously. At last, His Majesty cleared his throat and announced in a deep authoritative voice, "Gallant knight, has this scourge, this devil, been thwarted?"

George pulled the sword away and replied, "That he has, Your Majesty."

The king continued, "Is he no longer a menace to this farm, village, or any surrounding province?"

George sheathed his sword and answered, "I believe he is no longer a threat to anyone present."

"Indeed," said Grahame as he stepped forward, then bowed to the crowd, "for I have learned the err of my vicious, vicious ways."

"Then I declare this battle over," the king announced. "Sir George is victorious!"

The crowd burst into uproarious applause. Kenny was relieved. They had fooled the entire town, and neither of his friends had been hurt in the process.

But then someone else stepped out onto the battlefield.

For you see, when Grahame stood up to take his bow, his tail slid out of the pitchfork—and that did not go unnoticed.

Porky's father stormed up, waving his arms madly. "Whoa! Hold on a minute!" he yelled. He picked up the pitchfork and held it over his head. The audience oohed.

"This WHOLE thing is a joke! It was rigged from the start! The old coot was never gonna kill that dragon!" he said, pointing at George. He rubbed the tines of the fork. "And this ain't no magical pitchfork! It's just painted gold!"

Kenny's heart was beating so hard all he could hear was *ba-bump, ba-bump, ba-bump*. Scanning the stage, he saw that his mom, Charlotte, and a scowling George were watching Porky's father. Finally his gaze met with Grahame's lemony, glowing eyes. For the first time, since they'd met on this hill all those nights ago, he saw genuine fear in them.

"Now I say we take responsibility for our own and finish this once and for all!" Porky's father shouted, pointing the pitchfork at Grahame's chest. "Who's with me?"

# *XIII. Performance of a Lifetime*

KENNY'S EYES WENT BIG. THE river-stones, the fiery feeling, the river itself, was ready to explode out of him. How could he let the villagers kill Grahame after all of this? He had no more chess moves, no more strategies, no more books to help him. . . .

"NO!" he yelped. "Don't kill him!" He bolted toward Grahame and placed himself between the pitchfork and the dragon. "He's my best friend in the world! He never hurt any one of you!"

Porky's father did not falter, "Git outta the way, kid—this devil has to be dealt with! That's a fact."

"Actually," Kenny's mother said, "the fact is, the boy's right. And you're going to have to go through both of us in order to get to him." She stood behind her son, between the pitchfork and the dragon.

"An' me, too," the wizard said, removing his hat and revealing the familiar face of Kenny's father. He took his place behind Kenny, next to his wife, and placed both his hands on his son's shoulders.

The audience was dead silent. Porky's father wavered a bit but held his ground.

Next, George and Charlotte took their place behind Kenny's parents. Now they were all standing between the weapon and Grahame.

"Of course they're all standin' here!" Porky's father shouted to the crowd. "This is part of their little show! But this monster *has* to die before he kills one of us!"

Then Porky himself walked up and stood next to Kenny. He said to his ruffian father, "It was a really cool battle. Do we hafta kill 'im, Pa?"

Porky's father blinked and stepped back.

Silence. Not even the crickets were chirping.

All Kenny could hear in his head was his own breathing, which panted in time with the sound of the dragon's immense heart, beating rapidly.

*Oh gosh,* Kenny thought. *Grahame's nervous. And when he's nervous—*

"Hic!"

The fireball puffed out of the dragon's mouth and engulfed Porky's dad. The dumbfounded lout stood there blinking, trying to comprehend what had just happened. All the hair had been singed off his body, and the tips of his ears were smoking.

From the back of the audience there came a hearty, loud laugh, and a single clapping. "Encore! Encore!"

Everyone turned and looked.

Walking down the center aisle was His Royal Majesty, the king. He was clapping excitedly and laughing aloud with his two sons. The jester joined in, whistling and cheering and shouting, "Encore! Encore!"

Kenny watched as the shouting spread throughout the entire crowd. Soon the hilltop was clamoring, "ENCORE! ENCORE! ENCORE!"

The throngs of townsfolk surged forward

onto the stage. They cheered and lifted George, Charlotte, Kenny's parents, and Kenny himself up onto their shoulders. They carried them all around the amphitheater, hurrahing and hailing the troupe. Kenny looked over at Grahame, his best friend in the world, and smiled. The dragon responded in kind with his familiar toothy grin, then loaded a group of kids onto his back and pranced about the amphitheater with the rest of the party.

The sun finally settled down below the hills, causing the clouds in the sky to fade to a deep red before cooling off into a lovely shade of lavender. All along the horizon, the little lamplights of Roundbrook flickered on, but no one noticed—they were up on Shepard's Hill, celebrating the performance of a lifetime.

# *XIV. A Favorable Outcome*

"PECKING ORDER," KENNY'S FATHER said the next morning as he walked up to his son and handed him the pitchfork. "When the true leader is revealed, then there's a new order."

It was the dawn after the big battle. The celebration had gone on late into the night, with Kenny and his friends reenacting bits and pieces of their performance for eager groups. Now they were all back on the hill, cleaning up the aftermath of the enormous party.

Of course, Porky's dad was nowhere to be found—but Porky was there. He turned out to be just as excited to see a real live dragon as Kenny had been, commenting that Grahame seemed much hairier and scruffier than he'd imagined. In fact, several of Kenny's classmates, along with Charlotte, had arrived to help tidy up the hilltop.

"Last night was a blast," Charlotte said, dropping the hilt from a broken toy sword into a garbage can. Fluttering her eyes and putting the back of her paw on her forehead, she continued, "I've always wanted to be a damsel in distress."

The little buck smiled.

"Ho, bantling!" Grahame said, sweeping his cave entrance. "It looks like George is back—and with a few friends." He pointed to the road, and there was the king's royal procession heading their way.

Kenny's mother and father joined their son as the coach reached the summit of the hill. The young knights flanked the carriage as the driver hopped down and opened the door. Out came the jester, the royal sons, George, and finally the king himself.

"Kenneth Rabbit," the king said as he approached the lad, "I had to stop by and speak with you before we head back home."

Kenny gulped, glancing over at George. "Y-you don't have to do anything to Grahame, do you?" he asked.

"Heavens no!" the king said with a smile. "I want you, all of you"—he gestured to the group—"to come to my palace and give your performance for the royal court."

Kenny's mother gasped. His father whistled.

"Wow! Cool!" Charlotte said.

Kenny blinked. He looked over at George. The old knight was beaming.

"My boys and I haven't had a good time like that in ages," the king added, "and George tells me this was all your doing. So what do you say, lad?"

Kenny turned and looked up at the dragon. "Sounds good to me. Grahame, what do you think?"

Grahame looked down at everyone, smiled his toothy grin, and said, "You know, those royal cooks can make desserts you didn't even know existed. Have you ever tasted Austrian Lattice Pie?"

# *And So . . .*

*That is how our story closes. Kenny and company did indeed travel to the king's castle, where they performed for a week to standing-room-only crowds. That is where I, the royal historian, was finally able to meet the young rabbit and his best friend who had entertained an entire kingdom.*

*They reveled with the court, visited the royal library, and tasted a variety of delicious foods (including Austrian Lattice Pie). Kenny's mom even made crème brûlée for the king!*

## *And So . . .*

*It was an experience Kenny would never forget.*

*When the troupe finally returned home to their little farming town of Roundbrook, they were welcomed back with a roaring, huge homecoming parade. The townsfolk greeted each and every one of them with congratulations and admiration because by this time the legend of their act had spread all across the land.*

*After that summer, things settled back down. Kenny continued to live with his parents, started back at school, did his chores on the farm, and even helped out at George's bookshop with Charlotte. For you see, the knight had been commissioned by His Majesty to travel about the countryside revising* The King's Royal Bestiary, *and Kenny was determined to help ensure that the research in this new edition was thorough and that the subjects were handled accurately.*

*The celebrated rabbit of Roundbrook spent the rest of his time with his friends, flying kites, painting sunsets, and acting out plays in the amphitheater that he and Grahame had built on the hilltop.*

One Sunday, on a cool autumn afternoon, the boy was riding his bicycle up to the summit of Shepard's

Hill. As he hopped off and leaned his bike against a willow tree, he spied his friend curled up in a ball, dozing at the entrance of his cave.

"Hey, Grahame," he called so as not to startle the dragon.

The great beast opened one large luminous eye, stretched, and let out a terrific yawn. Smacking his lips, he said, "Bantling! I was just catching forty winks in this warm sunny spot I found on the rocks here. What's going on?"

"Mom's serving dinner early tonight," Kenny said, pulling something out of his satchel. "George and Charlotte are already there, so I thought I'd come up to get you. I wanted to show you this, too. It's a new book I borrowed."

The dragon sat right up, rubbing his scaly paws together. "Ooh, hand it over! I can't wait to see what it is—more prehistoric animals? Creatures from the Ice Age? Renaissance poetry, perhaps?"

Kenny handed the slim volume to him. "Naw, some fairy tale by a British guy. George said we'd really like it. Take a look."

"*The Reluctant Dragon*," Grahame read as he set his glasses on the bridge of his nose. "I like the title already . . . oh look, nice pictures!"

"Come on," Kenny said, heading back toward his bike. "Let's go get dinner and we'll start reading it tonight."

The dragon tucked the book and glasses into his cave and followed the boy to the tree where his bike was parked. "Sounds like a grand plan to me. What's your mom got on the menu tonight?"

"Um, soufflé, glazed carrots, and I think she's making the king's Austrian Lattice Pie for dessert, so we . . ."

"What are we waiting for, then?" the dragon squealed. He unfolded his expansive wings and began flapping them excitedly. "Race ya home!"

As they took off down the hill, the rabbit and the dragon, their laughter could be heard dancing and swirling about on the wind.